JOHNNY ALCORN

REMBRANDT'S BERET

OR THE PAINTER'S CROWN

PAINTINGS BY

STEPHEN ALCORN

Tambourine Books · New York

"You are supposed to be looking at me," said Grandfather Tiberius, "not at the boy on the wall. If you keep turning your head, Marie, I shall get your features all mixed up. Rembrandt would disapprove."

"But Grandpapa I *am* looking at you when I look at the boy on the wall. His eyes glow like yours. And that's your big, floppy beret. Who painted your portrait?"

"Sit still and pose. I shall tell you as I work."

It was almost a lifetime ago, on a cold autumn day right here in Florence. I was just about your age.

It all began when a great storm burst upon me as I walked home from school. The rain emptied the streets of people and filled them with puddles as big as ponds. The wind swirled through the squares and made the church bells swing wildly, filling the air with whistle and clang. My cape became a sail, and I was blown off course. I took cover in the first open doorway I saw.

Inside, two men stood chatting at the foot of a staircase that rose with no end in sight. One looked like a guard, and he called the other Sir Curator. The guard turned to me and said, "And what are you up to young man? We are closing soon for the siesta."

Before I could answer or escape, Sir Curator said, "Don't discourage the boy." With a sweep of his hand he told me, "Don't just stand there. Go up and see the pictures!" As I climbed the stairs I heard him call after me, "But hurry. We're leaving as soon as the rain lets up."

I paused at the top of the stairs. I was the only living soul about. It wasn't lonely, though. There were statues and paintings *everywhere*. At first one door seemed to lead to another, but soon I was lost.

A sign read Hall of the Old Masters—Special Admittance Only. From a window, on my tiptoes, I could see goldsmiths' shops and the swollen river blanketed by fog.

The whole town was asleep for the siesta. Everything seemed cozy and in its place. But I was soon reminded that something was very much out of place—*me*. For whom do I see strolling across the empty bridge below but Sir Curator and the guard! They had forgotten all about me. I was marooned for the afternoon.

Talk about Special Admittance! Feeling very curious and a little scared, I entered the Hall of the Old Masters.

There I was, all alone and surrounded by faces. I stared at them.

They stared back.

"I was framed! This endless posing is cruel and unusual punishment," came a voice from my right. Caravaggio! I remembered hearing shadowy stories about him—the daring young painter who was always getting into trouble.

"At least the child is not blathering about us the way adults do. As if we paintings could not speak for ourselves," came a voice from my left—Rubens, the famous painter-ambassador.

"The poor boy is frightened. He is as trapped as we are. Let us welcome him as a friend," said the one in the middle. His face was a battlefield marked by many skirmishes without victors or vanquished. He was Rembrandt van Rijn.

I thought I was imagining things. I started to retreat. How long and narrow the hall seemed as I tried to hurry without drawing attention to myself!

"Why do you run from your imagination?" boomed a voice from behind me. I recognized the voice of Rembrandt and stopped in my tracks. A rustle swept through the hall as each and every painter strained his neck from the canvas to see what I would do.

I simply stood there. Lo and behold, Caravaggio leapt down from his frame like a cat on the prowl. Then, without a word but with many a grunt, they all climbed from their frames. A few feet can be a great distance for a grown man if it is straight up or down. Somehow, jumping, spilling, dropping, diving, they all reached solid ground. I had to laugh.

For several moments no one spoke. Perhaps they were embarrassed. Perhaps it was not clear who should speak first among peers. Rubens broke the ice by musing, "So much for speaking for ourselves." At that they all laughed and the hall was filled with conversation.

The artists gathered round me in a circle. It was like a clearing in a brightly colored autumn forest. They towered above me in their extravagant clothes, and each held a palette dotted with pigments and long brushes richly tipped with mixed colors. The smells of turpentine, linseed oil, and varnish swept over me.

They introduced themselves with a bow and a flourish: Michelangelo, Leonardo, Raffaello, Tiziano . . . the names kept rolling like waves. I bowed as best I could and told them my name. "Oh, Tiberius!" said Rembrandt, "you have an ancient and glorious name like my beloved son Titus. You resemble him in more than name." They all agreed, and I knew I was welcome among them.

Rembrandt stepped forward. His eyes glowed like embers. "We pass our days gazing upon our portraits, lingering over what we have done and been." He paused. A smile spread across his face as he said, "Enough with our masks. We must paint a face of promise instead."

"Aye! Aye!" said one and all. Their hearts were pounding.

I sensed that Rembrandt longed to paint one more time. He gambled on his wish. "Let us pool our brushes and have Tiberius pick one. The owner of the chosen brush will paint Tiberius' portrait."

I found myself looking at a dazzling bouquet of brushes. My finger flitted around it like a bee as I tried to make up my mind. Rembrandt looked me straight in the eye. I saw a brush tipped with a blazing daub of gold pigment: the color of Rembrandt's chain. I let my finger fall on it. Rembrandt and I had tricked chance.

"I need one more thing: a canvas to paint on," said Rembrandt.

"There are rolls of the finest linen canvas in the storage room," said Caravaggio with a gleam in his eye. "I saw it as I was being carried to the restorer's workshop." Off we went to the storage room. While Rembrandt cut and stretched a piece of canvas, the others rummaged through the clutter of homeless paintings.

"Good grief! Here's one of mine!" cried Rubens. "Why isn't it hanging!?" Everyone laughed. Then Caravaggio held up a newfangled painting by Picasso for all to see.

"Poor Picasso," said Rubens, "it looks like his model just wouldn't sit still."

"Now, now, Rubens," said Caravaggio. "*This* should be hanging. This Picasso has invented a bold, new way to do what we do—show things inside out."

"I am ready," said Rembrandt.

"Rembrandt, let Tiberius wear your plumed beret—the painter's crown," said Rubens.

"I'm not used to painting without it, but if you insist . . ." said Rembrandt.

THE PAINTER'S CROWN: The words kept echoing in my ears as Rembrandt placed his enormous cap on my head.

"Without your beret, Rembrandt, you look like a lion," remarked Rubens, "and the lion is a king who needs no crown." A hush came over the room as Rembrandt laid out his colors, and everyone left to wander the museum while Rembrandt painted my portrait.

"*Voilà!*" said Rubens, peering in from the door. Rembrandt held the finished portrait up for me to see, the way a barber holds a mirror after a haircut. I saw my reflection in the canvas, an image surprising yet true.

All the painters praised Rembrandt's work for quite a while, but Rembrandt said nothing until Rubens asked, "What will you name the picture? *Portrait of Tiberius?*"

"No," answered Rembrandt. "Tiberius has silently asked a thousand questions with his eyes, just like a painter. I shall call it *Portrait of the Artist as a Very, Very Young Man,* and give Tiberius the brushes with which I painted it."

We heard a heavy thump downstairs—the bolt on the great door. The museum was open again. Rembrandt quickly took my hand and said, "On behalf of my immortal colleagues, farewell and good luck. May your memory serve you well."

Caravaggio boosted his fellows up into their frames. He was tempted to remain at large, but leapt to his frame muttering, "I, too, am a slave to immortality."

I suddenly realized I still had Rembrandt's beret on. "Rembrandt, your painter's crown!" I cried.

"Shush, they'll hear you," he whispered. "Keep my beret, and wear it at all times. It will keep your imagination from escaping." They waved a great wave and, like the ocean after a storm, receded.

I tucked my portrait under my cape and hoped that no one would notice that a piece of canvas was missing. I retraced my steps and went downstairs the fast way—sliding on the banister! The guard saw me and hollered, "Sorry we forgot about you! It's a lonely place, isn't it!" What if he saw my portrait? I was terrified.

As I whizzed by I could just imagine Caravaggio roaring in laughter at my predicament, and one more skirmish of hope and worry etched on Rembrandt's face.

But it was clear sailing all the way out!

As my mother marveled at my portrait, I told her how I had met Rembrandt, and I told it all in one breath. She said she didn't believe me. But maybe she did, in her own way. The next day when I came home from school I found a set of artists' colors, a palette, and a roll of canvas on my bed. An easel stood in the corner. And I still have Rembrandt's brushes.

And that is how I became a painter.

"I've never seen you without Rembrandt's beret, Grandpapa."

"Well, I'm no lion. *Voilà!* Your portrait is finished."

"It's beautiful. Am I really that pretty?"

"You're too modest, Marie."

"Maybe I'll paint your portrait someday, Grandpapa."

"I hope so, Marie. That would be a dream come true for me, and a jewel in my painter's crown. I shall give you Rembrandt's brushes. . . . Rembrandt would surely approve."

In Florence, Italy, two of the world's great museums, the Uffizi Gallery and the Pitti Palace, are linked by a serpentine passageway that spans the Arno River above the goldsmiths' shops on the Ponte Vecchio. The passageway is graced with portraits and self-portraits of the Old Masters: Leonardo da Vinci, Michelangelo Buonarroti, Peter Paul Rubens, Raffaello Sanzio (Raphael), Tiziano Vecellio (Titian), and many more. An especially fine self-portrait by Rembrandt van Rijn crowns the collection.

Seek out paintings by the Old Masters in museums and in books. They will speak to you.

Library of Congress Cataloging in Publication Data
Alcorn, Johnny. Rembrandt's beret / by Johnny Alcorn; pictures by Stephen Alcorn. p.   cm.
Summary: Tiberius tells how the paintings came alive one day in a museum and Rembrandt painted a picture of Tiberius and gave him his beret and his brushes.
[1. Painting—Fiction.   2. Rembrandt Harmenszoon van Rijn, 1606–1669—Fiction.]   I. Alcorn, Stephen, ill.   II. Title.
PZ7.A3345Re 1991 [Fic]—dc20   90–42330 CIP AC
ISBN 0-688-10206-9—ISBN 0-688-10207-7 (lib. bdg.)
Printed in Italy by L.E.G.O.
First edition
1 3 5 7 9 10 8 6 4 2